WANNEROO		
1 6 MAR 2011		
Burrows 3/11		
Seddon 19/4		
M. Henderson 6/12		
N. Tolkien 5/16		
5/17		
3/18 3/20 BEAUTIFUL		

SAD SONG

Vincent Banville

BBC
LARGE
PRINT

First published in 1999 by
New Island
This Large Print edition published
2010 by BBC Audiobooks by
arrangement with
New Island

ISBN 978 1 405 62301 8

British Library Cataloguing in Publication Data available

Printed and bound in Great Britain by
CPI Antony Rowe, Chippenham and Eastbourne

CHAPTER ONE

Blaine was all done up like a dog's dinner. He was wearing his tan suit, with a lime-green shirt. A purple handkerchief flowed from the top pocket. His shoes were black and laced, his chin was shaved, his hair combed. He was neat, clean and well-shined. He was calling on one million pounds.

More than a million, if the truth were told. James J. Carey was a 'cute hoor' from the West of Ireland. He had started in the building trade in a small way. First a wheelbarrow. Then a push-cart. Then a lorry that wouldn't start when it rained. In the 1960s he had moved to London. There he joined up with another Mayo man called McMullen. They laid tar in peoples' driveways. They built sheds and cut corners whenever they could. The business went well.

They began to make money. Then McMullen fell—or was he pushed?—into a giant cement mixer and became part of a pedestrian crossing in Earl's Court.

Carey married his widow and took over the running of the entire business. Things went so well that in the 1990s he was able to come back to Dublin and run his empire from there. Now he was one of the richest men in Ireland. When he sent for someone, that someone broke into a gallop to come and see him.

So Blaine moved fast. Since he had set up as a private detective, work had been scarce. Before that he had been in insurance, but the job bored him. His hurling career with Wexford had not gone well either. Three All-Ireland finals and each of them lost. Also, his wife Annie had left him for a body-builder called Harold. It would be true to say that he was a bit down. But when the call had come from Carey, he thought he might soon see light at the end of the tunnel.

It was a beautiful June day as he hurried along the quays. The smell from the Liffey was awful. The Carey building was huge, like a giant mushroom against the sky. Twelve steps up, swing doors. A porter with a stare like a red-hot poker. A girl who looked as if she had been shined all over sat behind a desk. Blaine spoke to her in hushed tones. She had nails long enough to slice a loaf of bread.

'Mr Carey is expecting you?' she asked, as though she didn't really believe him.

'At sixteen minutes past the hour,' Blaine said. 'I was told to be on time.'

The girl pressed a button set into the desk. A minute went by, then another female, who could have been the girl's twin, appeared.

'Follow me,' she told Blaine, and led him down a corridor.

At the end was a large double door. She pushed one side of it open and waved to Blaine to go in. He moved smartly inside and the door whispered softly shut behind him. If she locked it, he would need a sledge hammer to get back out again.

CHAPTER TWO

The office was large enough to land a helicopter. Carey sat behind a desk that was about an acre in area. He had hair like steel wool. A tanned face. Eyes as cold as winter frost. And a small mouth as tight as a duck's arse. His voice had a smoker's edge to it when he spoke.

'You're Blaine?'

'I was the last time I looked in a mirror.'

Carey frowned.

'Cut out the smart remarks. I want you to find my daughter Sam and bring her home.'

'Sam?'

'Her mother gave her the name Assumpta, but she hates it. So everyone calls her Sam.'

'Johnny Cash had a song about a boy called Sue.'

'What's that got to do with anything?'

'Just making conversation.'

'You're not here to make conversation. How long will it take you to find her?'

'Depends on where she is.'

'Last I heard she was living in a squat with a crowd of drop-outs. Here's a photograph of her.'

Carey poked the snap across his desk and Blaine had to hurry to catch it before it fell on the floor. It was a colour head-and-shoulders shot of an open-faced, cheerful-looking girl. She was in her late teens or early twenties.

'Maybe I should talk to her mother,' Blaine suggested.

'Her mother departed . . .'

'She passed over to the other side?' Blaine asked, wondering if he should bless himself.

'Only to the other side of Dublin. She divorced me a couple of years ago.'

'Oh.'

'The address of where she's been living up to recently is on the back of the photo. Somewhere in Cabra.'

'The mother?'

'No, the daughter.'

'Why don't you go and bring her back yourself?'

'I'm too busy. That's why I hire people like you.'

'I charge two-hundred-and-fifty a day. Plus expenses.'

'See Sylvia on the way out. She'll give you a cheque for five days' work. That should be enough for a simple job like this.'

'What if Sam doesn't want to come home?'

'Persuade her. Put a rope around

her and drag her back if you have to. A daughter's place is by her father's side. Not living the life of a down-and-out.'

Carey pressed a button—it was a great place for button pressing. The same girl who had shown Blaine in now appeared to show him out. She didn't speak to him. Just marched ahead, while he followed along behind, admiring the sway of her bottom. It was worth watching.

CHAPTER THREE

Blaine got in his car, an old Renault that used diesel and sounded like a tank. He drove to Cabra. He was looking for Number Thirteen, Feltrim Road. A girl with orange hair and vampire eyes gave him directions, which turned out to be wrong.

He started again, asking directions

from an old man pushing a bicycle. This time he was put right. The road had two rows of neat houses with postage-stamp lawns. Number Thirteen had an uncared-for look about it, like a bad tooth in a set of shining dentures.

He locked his car, pushed open a rusty gate and walked up to the front door. He knocked and, after some time went by, the door was opened. An eye like a blood sunset appeared in the crack.

'Sam Carey, sometimes known as Assumpta?' Blaine inquired somewhat doubtfully.

The door opened more fully, to reveal a thin young man in a vest and dirty jeans. He had a large hooped earring in his right ear, yellow hair and a sneer on his face.

'Yarahhh,' he said in a voice that sounded as if he needed to spit. Blaine sighed, said a silent prayer, then moved forward into the hallway. The young man went backwards,

8

surprised.

'I'm looking for a girl named Sam Carey,' Blaine explained patiently. 'I was told she lived here. If she's on the premises, I'd like to talk to her. If she has moved on, I'd be grateful if you'd give me her address.'

'Moved on,' Yellow Hair said. 'What you want her for?'

'She bought a ticket in a draw. She's won a Barbie doll and I'm here to deliver.'

'Where is it then?'

'She's got no clothes on, so I left her in the car.'

'Yarahhh,' Yellow Hair said again, and this time he did spit, just missing Blaine's shoe.

Blaine lost patience, reached out and stuck his right index finger through Yellow Hair's earring. With his other hand he caught the guy by the throat. Pulling firmly on the earring, he said, 'Just give me the girl's present whereabouts, and you'll have two ears to listen with for the rest of your life.'

The guy opened and shut his mouth like a fish out of water. His eyes bulged as Blaine pulled a little harder on the earring. 'She's doing up an old warehouse in Ringsend,' he gasped. 'Her and a crowd of students.'

'There now, that wasn't too hard, was it?' Blaine said. He released his hold on Yellow Hair's throat and gave the earring one more tug for luck.

'Hey, what you want to do that for?' the guy protested.

'Pain is good for the soul,' Blaine told him. 'Maybe you'll be more polite the next time.'

'There isn't going to be a next time, I'm out of here.'

'Me too,' Blaine said, and he turned, walked back down the path, got in his car and drove away.

CHAPTER FOUR

The sun was high in the sky as Blaine drove along the quays in the direction of Ringsend. June 16th, the day in 1904 that a Jew named Bloom walked around Dublin and became famous. Blaine glanced in his rear-view mirror. He didn't see Bloom, but he did spy a bright red van that appeared to be following him since he left Cabra. Then again, maybe he was just imagining it. He visited a number of empty warehouses before he finally found the one he was looking for. It stood by itself, right on the edge of the quayside. If you walked out the back door, you'd find yourself swimming in Dublin Bay.

Scaffolding had been set up against the front of the building, and a fellow and a girl were painting the frontage black. Blaine parked his car and walked in under them. A sign on the door explained that the place was being prepared as a centre for refugees. The inside was huge and had an echo. An Abba tape was playing. The girls were singing about 'Money, money, money in a rich man's world.' A number of young people were doing various things: painting, hammering, drilling holes in walls. Blaine was deafened by the noise. He went back outside, where he leaned against the side of the building and lit a cigarette. The river flowed full and smooth. A tugboat honked. Seagulls screamed. The sky was a pale blue, with just a rinse of white cloud. He smoked for a while, then he turned and glanced back down the quays. The red van was parked some distance away. A bright flash of sunlight glanced off the windscreen, but he was pretty sure there were two people in the front seats. He finished the cigarette, threw it away and went back inside the warehouse. The crowd of workers was taking a break. The tape had been switched off. He went across to the nearest group. They stared at him curiously. The girl he was looking for was not among them.

'Sam Carey?' he inquired.

'Who's asking?' Blaine gazed at the fat young man with glasses who answered him.

'I'm a friend of the family,' he said. 'Just calling in to say hello.'

'As I hear it, Sam doesn't get on with her family.'

'Surely she has a favourite uncle?'

'And you're him?'

'I might be.'

The guy looked at the girl sitting beside him. She shrugged her shoulders, then said, 'Sam's in the office. Up the stairs. Door facing you.'

Blaine nodded his thanks and followed her directions. Some of the steps on the stairs were loose and creaked under his weight. He walked along the short corridor at the top and knocked on the closed door. A voice told him to come in. He did so. There were two people inside. A girl and a boy. Blaine did not have to take out the photo to see that the girl was Sam Carey. She was wearing a bright orange bandanna around her hair, a striped T-shirt and paint-streaked cream overalls. Her eyes smiled. The guy with her was big and strong, with muscles that bulged through his singlet. He was wearing cut-off denim shorts that showed his muscular legs. He was also wearing a look on his face that told Blaine to watch his step. Otherwise he might be going back down the stairs head-first.

CHAPTER FIVE

'Yes?' Sam Carey said, the smile beginning to fade from her eyes. 'You wanted something?'

14

Blaine leaned a shoulder against the door jamb and tried to look pleasant. He said, 'My name's John Blaine. I've been hired by your father to find you. And to ask you politely if you'll come home.'

'How polite will you be if she says no?' the guy with the muscles asked.

'Save it, Artie,' the girl said. 'Let's handle this with kid gloves.' She and the guy had been examining what looked like plans of the building, set out on a table. Now she plopped into a chair, then pointed at another one facing her. 'Why don't you sit down?' she said to Blaine. 'There's something I need to explain to you.'

'Explain nothing,' Artie said, flexing his muscles. 'Why don't you let me throw this geezer out of here?'

'Because that'll solve nothing. Either he'll come back or someone else will.' The girl put a hand on Artie's arm and squeezed gently. 'Maybe if you went and got yourself a cup of coffee? I'll deal with this.'

Artie put on his sulky look, but he did as he was told. As he went past Blaine he managed to give him a shove with his hip. Blaine's fifteen stone of muscle and just a little fat refused to budge. This annoyed Artie even more and he nearly took the door off the hinges as he went out.

'Do you mind if I smoke?' Blaine asked, moving forward and sitting down on the chair in front of the girl.

'I'll join you,' she said. She took a long, thin Russian cigarette out of a packet and waited while Blaine held a light to it before lighting his own. They blew smoke at one another, then the girl said, 'I haven't seen you before. You must be new.'

'Your father makes a habit of sending people to bring you home?'

She nodded, then carefully picked a flake of tobacco off her bottom lip. She had a nice mouth, made for smiling. She also had a nice figure. Since Annie had left him, Blaine had been on lean rations where dealings with the opposite sex were concerned. Sam Carey was a bit young for him, but there was no harm in looking. She took another puff on her cigarette, then stubbed it out in an ashtray made from a large sea-shell. She said, 'My father has a number of people working for him. Some of them are pretty tough. Are you tough?'

'No,' Blaine said, grinning at her, 'I'm as harmless as a soft toy.'

'You don't look harmless. How did you get the scar over your eye?'

'An old hurling injury. I've a few more, but I'd have to take off some clothes to show them to you.'

'Maybe later. If we get to know one another better.'

'You think there's a chance of that?'

'I wouldn't bet on it.'

Blaine leaned across the table and dropped some ash in the sea-shell. He said, 'Tell me why you keep running away from home. Does your father beat you?'

'No, but he does want me to do something against my will.'

'And that is?'

Before the girl could answer, there was a sudden outbreak of noise from downstairs. Then Artie came bursting in the door, almost knocking Blaine off his chair. 'What is it?' the girl asked him.

'Jimbo here brought company. There's a crowd of your father's goons below, and they haven't come to help us paint the place. We've got to get you out of here.'

CHAPTER SIX

Blaine, who had stood up from his chair, now moved back a pace as Artie came at him, fists at the ready. 'Hold on a minute,' said Blaine. 'I give you my word I brought no one with me. They must have followed me here. I did spot a red van behind me.'

'Red van me arse,' Artie told him. 'I'll break you in little bits.'

Sensing that the time for talking was over, Blaine swung his leg and brought his foot with some force up between Artie's denim-clad thighs. There was a satisfying thud—for Blaine but not for Artie—and the muscular hero bent over and bit the dust. 'I should have warned him I don't fight fair,' Blaine muttered. 'Always protect your essentials.'

'You didn't have to do that,' Sam said, bending over the fallen Artie.

'He said he was going to break me into little pieces.'

'He may have said it, but he didn't mean it.'

'You could have fooled me.' Blaine helped the girl lift Artie up and put him sitting in a chair. He had gone a very odd colour, and all that could be seen of his eyes were the whites.

19

'He'll be OK in a little while,' Blaine said. 'When he gets his breath back.'

'I hope you haven't ruined his chances of marriage.'

'Why, are you engaged to him?'

'No, we're just good friends.' Blaine cocked his ear to listen to the sounds of battle downstairs. 'Sounds as if your pals are giving a good account of themselves,' he said. 'They must be used to fighting for your honour by now.'

'They do what they can to protect me.'

'Is there any other way out of here, other than by the front door?'

'Not unless you want to swim for it.'

'It's a bit early in the year for me to go in swimming.'

'Then I guess we'll just have to take the boat.'

'The boat?'

'I keep a boat moored to the back door, just in case. I don't know why I'm telling you that, though, if you're with them.'

'Didn't I give you my word I'm not? And my word is my bond.'

'As in James Bond?'

'Can't you see that I'm shaken, but not stirred?'

'Right, follow me.' The girl turned to go, then looked back at the winded Artie. He had got his colour back and was beginning to show signs of life. 'You're sure he'll be all right?'

'Yeah. Maybe a twinge or two when he goes pee-pee, but that'll pass.'

'Let's go then.'

Blaine followed the girl out the door. As he passed the seated Artie he gave him a whack on the ear, just to keep his mind off his other trouble below the waist.

CHAPTER SEVEN

Blaine followed Sam Carey to another door in the top corridor. This led to an iron stairway that ran down the back of the building. At the bottom there was a small cement jetty, with a rowboat tied to it. They got in, Blaine at the back, the girl in the middle manning the oars. She obviously knew what she was about, for the boat surged from the warehouse like a greyhound out of the traps.

She rowed out to the middle of the bay, then let the oars trail in the water. The afternoon was still warm, the bay calm, like a pond. A large tanker was moored to the opposite wharf. A naval vessel sat a little way from it. A bell tolled and the heavy notes rolled across the water. 'Peaceful isn't it?' the girl said. 'I sometimes come out here like this and just sit and stare.'

'I'm not a very good sailor,' Blaine told her. 'When I was at university I worked on the mail-boat between Rosslare and Fishguard for the summer. My job was to make toast for the passengers. Even when the boat was moored at the dock I got sea-sick.'

'I love the sea. It's one of my ambitions to sail round the world.'

'And your father is stopping you from doing that?'

'Worse than that. He wants me to get married.'

'Fathers are like that. They want their daughters settled down and raising daughters of their own.'

'You sound as if you're a father yourself.'

'No, but I had hopes. Then my wife left me.'

'Why?'

'Why did she leave me? Probably a million reasons.'

'Didn't you love one another?'

'Yes, but sometimes love isn't enough. I probably asked too much of her. She needed her own space. Room to live.'

'Like me. Freedom. To experience everything. Starting with free love.'

'Love isn't free. It costs, just like everything else. Life is a bit of a sad song, really. Certainly more sadness than joy.'

Sam shook her head, her face serious.

'I don't believe that,' she said. 'You shape it the way you want. Not the way someone else wants it for you.'

'We're back to your father again?'

The girl took the packet of Russian cigarettes from her pocket and offered one to Blaine. He took it and lit it before passing the lighter to Sam. The boat rocked when he moved and he quickly settled himself again.

A curious seagull hovered, throwing his shadow across the water. On the tanker a man wearing a baseball cap leaned over the rail, whistling tunelessly.

'Let me tell you about my father,' Sam said, her face grim. 'Then maybe you won't be so eager to bring me back to him.'

CHAPTER EIGHT

'I'm an only child,' the girl said, sitting quietly and puffing at her cigarette. 'When I was fifteen, my mother left home and divorced my father. Custody of me went to him, because my mother has a drink problem. My father had very little time for me. He's the old-fashioned type. Thinks women should be seen and not heard. There was a number of mistresses. Girls only a little older than me. I was more or less left to myself.'

'I suppose you were sent to an expensive boarding school?'

'That's right. I'm a shy person and I was very lonely. The nuns couldn't help. They had no experience of life. But I'm also stubborn. I decided to get on with things as best I could. Up to recently, my father had no interest in me. Then suddenly he began hinting that I should settle down and get married.'

'Was there a reason for this?'

'Of course. I became suspicious and did a bit of poking around in his affairs. I found out that he had made a number of bad moves in his business. Paying money for huge contracts and then not getting them. It seems the only way to save himself was to join up with another company. One called Stoneroad. It's owned by a man named Mulligan. Now Mulligan has a son, a right half-wit, who spends his time drinking, gambling and fighting. Mulligan wants him to settle down and take an interest in the business. And the first step would be for him to take a wife.'

'Aha,' Blaine said. 'Light dawns. It would suit Mulligan and your father if the two of you got hitched. Mulligan's son would get a nice respectable wife, and the joining of the two companies would put your father's business back in the black.'

'Exactly.'

'Pretty cold-blooded. For a father to treat his only daughter like that.'

'Well, there's a chance that he's not really my father at all.'

'Oh?'

'My mother was married before. To a man called McMullen. He had an accident and was killed. She married Carey very soon afterwards. But they never got on. Then there was a rumour that she had an affair with one of Carey's foremen, a man named George Emerson. But he also died in an accident. Now and then my mother dropped hints that this Emerson might have been my father. But she would never come out and tell me the whole truth.'

Blaine flipped the butt of his cigarette in the water and watched it float away. He looked back at the girl. 'I can see how your life has been fairly complicated,' he said. 'I wish there was something I could do to help you. But I've taken Carey's money.'

'Spend it. Then go back and tell him you couldn't find me.'

'But the guys who followed me will tell him that I did find you. Why do you think he sent them after me?'

'Because he doesn't trust anyone. Even himself. I'll bet his right hand doesn't know what the left hand is up to.'

'Have you a safe place to stay while I see if I can do something?'

'Artie has a flat.'

'I don't think Artie would be too happy to see me.' Blaine paused, then he said, 'I've a house on the Cabra Road. You could stay there while I go and see Carey. Maybe talk some sense into him.'

'The only way you could do that is to beat him over the head with a chair leg.'

'So?'

'Would I be safe in your house?'

'Carey doesn't know where I live.'

'I don't mean from him. From you.'

Blaine grinned. 'Didn't I tell your friends that I was your favourite uncle? Can you be safer than that?'

CHAPTER NINE

They stayed out in the bay for a while longer. Then the girl rowed them in at an angle to where they had started out. The boat safely tied up, they went back in the direction of the warehouse. A little way along, a van that had once been red passed them, going very slowly. The vehicle had been sprayed with various coloured paints so that it looked like

29

a moving rainbow.

'Your friends obviously won the battle,' Blaine said. 'Quite a nice bit of artwork.'

They got his car and drove up the North Circular and onto the Cabra Road. Blaine's house was old and run-down. The garden was like a jungle. 'You could hide a tribe of apes in here,' Sam said, brushing a trailing branch out of her way.

'If you're lucky you might see Tarzan swinging through the trees.'

'I wouldn't be at all surprised.'

Blaine unlocked the door, then had to push hard because of the pile of mail on the floor behind it. 'Don't you live here?' the girl asked him.

'Now and then. The letters are mostly bills. I leave them there in the hope that they'll blow away in the wind.'

They went along the hall into the kitchen that looked exactly like a war zone. Dirty dishes were everywhere. And the remains of a take-away festered in the middle of the table.

'Must be the butler's day off,' Sam observed. She went to the fridge and opened it, then just as quickly shut it. 'There's something dead in there,' she said. 'And it wasn't yesterday that it died, but last week.'

'If I'd known you were coming, I would have cleared up a bit. When you live on your own, you're inclined to get a bit careless.'

'Is the rest of the house in as bad a state as this?'

'Why don't you explore a bit and find out? I'll make some tea.'

'Don't drink tea. How about a Coke?'

Blaine found a tin of Budweiser and a Pepsi. They took them into the sitting room and sat down. This room had a very nice mantelpiece, but the carpet on the floor looked as if it had been chewed by furry animals.

'This armchair smells of dog,' Sam said, wrinkling her nose.

'My wife Annie had a pet poodle. Name of Claude. He hated me, and I hated him.'

'Was he the cause of her leaving you?'

'One of them. She also thought I should get a proper job. One that would bring in a steady income.'

'What is your job?'

'Didn't I tell you? I'm a private dick.'

The girl spluttered into her Pepsi. 'Is that a first cousin to a Peeping Tom?'

'Very funny,' Blaine said. 'What I mean is that I've set up as a private detective. Mostly I find people.'

'Like you found me.'

'It wasn't difficult.'

Sam finished her drink, then got up and stood looking out the window.

'I won't stay here long,' she said. 'So if you're going to Carey, you'd better get a move on. I don't think it'll do any good, but it's decent of you to try.'

'I'll take a chair leg with me,' Blaine said standing up. 'If all else fails, I'll brain him.'

CHAPTER TEN

Blaine was about to get into his car when another old banger drew up, blocking his way. The engine kept running after it was switched off, then it suddenly stopped with an almighty bang. A cloud of blue smoke made him cough.

He went out to the gate and watched his wife Annie get out of the driver's side. She had tightly curled hair, freckles and a figure an artist would have given his eye-teeth to paint nude. She was wearing an open-necked shirt and jeans. She didn't seem surprised to see him.

'Hi, I've come for my sewing machine. And a few other bits and pieces.'

'How have you been? I've missed you.'

'I've missed you too.'

'Then why don't you come back and clean the bloody house? It's like a tip-head.'

The smile left Annie's face, to be replaced by a scowl. She raised a clenched fist.

'Get out of my way or I'll sock you one in the eye. And hire a maid if you want the house cleaned.'

'Annie, I'm sorry,' Blaine said. 'That didn't come out the way it was meant to. I miss you for yourself.'

'Is that so? Then who may I ask is the female staring out the window at us? I hope she's your solicitor and that you're getting ready for a divorce.'

Blaine turned and saw Sam Carey at the window. She gave him a little wave.

'That's a client of mine,' he explained, turning back to Annie.

34

'She needs a place to hide out for a while. Her father wants her to marry someone she's not in love with.'

'Funny, the same thing happened to me.'

Blaine took a pace back, as if she had indeed hit him.

'You don't mean that,' he said. 'You know you love me. It's just that at the moment you don't particularly like me. There is a difference, you know.'

'I know, I know, I know.' Annie's voice went up on each word. She was beginning to look upset.

'But I'm not in the mood for this kind of thing at the moment. We need to meet and talk.'

'So when?'

'When what?'

'When will we meet to talk?'

Blaine gazed at her, his mouth open. Then he closed it and said, 'Look I have to be somewhere. I'll call you and we'll arrange to have dinner. Somewhere nice and quiet and romantic.'

'Nice and quiet will do. Forget the romantic bit.'

'Do you still go all wobbly when I kiss you?'

Annie dodged around him and went in along the drive. Over her shoulder she said, 'Don't think I'm going to give you the chance to find out. Hell will freeze over before I'll allow you to kiss me, buster.'

Blaine watched her go, the grin back on his face. Then the grin faded when he realised her car was still blocking his way. With a resigned shrug he went to get her so that she could move it.

CHAPTER ELEVEN

Blaine parked on double yellow lines outside Carey's mushroom-shaped building. He placed his 'Doctor on Call' sign against the windscreen, then went inside, whistling. The same polished female was sitting at the same table in the foyer. Blaine gave her a nod, then made for the stairs.

As he put his foot on the first step, her voice cut into his back like a thrown dart.

'Where do you think you're going?'

He turned and looked back over his shoulder at her.

'I've important information to convey to Mr Carey.'

'About what?'

'About his daughter, whom he has hired me to find.'

'And have you?'

'Have I what?'

'Have you found her?'

'That is for Boss Carey to know and you to find out. Have you got his ear?'

'What?'

'Does he tell you his secrets?'

'Of course not.'

'Then neither shall I.'

With a toss of his head, Blaine continued on up the stairs, while the woman at the desk stared after him. She had a faraway look on her face, as though trying to work out a difficult problem in her mind. Blaine walked up to the door of Carey's office and knocked. He waited a moment, then pushed it open and went inside. A large guy with a strangely coloured head was standing in front of the desk. When he turned to see who had come in, Blaine saw that he had been sprayed with a variety of paints.

'I just can't keep up with the latest fashion,' Blaine said to him. 'First it was earrings, then nose rings and now this. Have you been sprayed all over or just your head?'

The guy frowned, then looked back at Carey, who was sitting behind the desk.

'This is the chump we followed to the warehouse,' he said. 'What's he doing here?'

'I don't know,' Carey told him. He gazed at Blaine. 'What are you doing here? Did you bring my daughter back?'

'I might have, if this chancer and his pals hadn't butted in. Why did you send them after me? I'm a big boy, you know. I don't have to have my hand held.'

'I'll do more than hold it,' the other guy said. 'I'll tear it off and shove it up your gable end.'

'That's enough, Alfred,' Carey said. 'Let's hear what he's got to say before we start jumping up and down on his head.'

Blaine smiled at Alfred, then he went to a chair at the side of the desk and sat down. He took out his cigarettes, put one in his mouth and lit it. He crossed his legs, leaned back, blew smoke at the ceiling.

'Mr Carey doesn't like people smoking in his office,' Alfred said.

'Tough.' Blaine flicked ash on the

carpet. 'Good for the pile,' he said, rubbing it in with his foot.

'I'll give you ten seconds to start talking,' Carey said in a tight voice. 'And it better be good. Otherwise I'll let Alfred loose on you.'

'He bites, does he?'

'You better believe it.'

'Right then, here goes . . .'

CHAPTER TWELVE

'I did find your daughter,' Blaine told Carey, 'and was having a pleasant conversation with her when your thugs came along and spoiled it all.'

'Alfred has just told me you went sailing out in the bay with her.'

'Not sailing, rowing.'

'Whatever.'

'She told me an interesting story. About how you're trying to get her to marry some bozo to save your business.'

'A pack of lies. The business is in great shape.'

'I think I'd prefer to believe her rather than you.'

'Believe what you like.' Carey leaned forward in his chair. 'Where is she now? Have you got her hidden away somewhere?'

'Not me. She took off when we got to shore.'

'Is that so? Then why aren't you out there looking for her? You're still in my employ.'

'No, I'm not. That ended when you sent your hard men to follow me.'

'You've got my money.'

'I gave it back,' Blaine lied. 'To the ice lady downstairs.'

'So what are you doing here, then?'

'I thought maybe I could talk some sense into you. Get you to act like a proper father. Respect your daughter's wishes and let her live her own life, as she chooses.'

Carey got up and came out from

behind his desk. He was tall and in good shape, considering his age. 'I could take you on,' he said to Blaine. 'But I've got guys working for me who do that kind of thing. Alfred here will conduct you off the premises. He might even give you a little gift to help you on your way. I don't want to see you again. Ever.'

Blaine stood up. He let his cigarette fall on the carpet and put his foot on it. He grinned at Carey. 'Seems like the end of a beautiful friendship,' he said. 'I was thinking of asking you out for some fishing. Or maybe a spot of golf . . .'

'Don't fish, don't golf.'

'Maybe Alfred does?'

Alfred eased in close to Blaine, then gave him a push.

'Move along, mutt,' he said. 'You're taking up space, where you shouldn't.'

Blaine walked to the door, Alfred in step with him. Before he went out, he turned and looked back at Carey.

'Leave Sam alone,' he said. 'Otherwise you'll have me to reckon with.'

'Big deal, little man,' Carey sneered. 'See that he gets a few thumps to remember me by,' he said to Alfred. 'But leave his kisser alone. Don't want someone with a marked face leaving the building. Bad for business.'

Blaine and his companion descended the stairs, then went down one more flight to the basement. There Alfred was joined by another two hard men, who held Blaine while Alfred whacked him in the ribs. By the time they pushed him back out onto the street, he felt as if he had gone rounds with Iron Mike Tyson.

CHAPTER THIRTEEN

Blaine went around to the front of the building. He thought about finding a brick and throwing it through one of the large front windows. He shook his head. 'There's more than one way to skin a cat,' he told himself.

He opened the door of his car and eased himself in painfully. Felt as if one rib, if not half a dozen, were broken. He drove down the quays, then into Amiens Street and along the North Strand. A friend of his called Leo Quinn lived in one of the tall old houses to his left. He found a spot and parked. Getting out of the car was even harder than getting in. He walked along the pavement, crouched over like the thousand-year-old man. Leo had a basement flat. Blaine went down the steps and knocked. He waited, then gave the door an almighty kick.

Putting his ear to the wood panel, he heard shuffling steps approaching. It was later in the evening now and he knew that Leo had probably started drinking. Leo was an alcoholic who had once trained to be a doctor. He never actually qualified but knew more about medicine than many a surgeon with letters after his name. He ran a practice from his flat, treating people who for one reason or another wouldn't go to a regular doctor. He did a thriving business.

The door squeaked open and Leo stood blinking in the evening sunlight. Someone had once said that Leo was so thin you could read a magazine through him. He had a narrow head with sparse sandy hair, faded blue eyes and a nose as red as a stop light. He was a sorry sight.

'Good evening, Doctor Spock,' Blaine said. 'I need to be taped up. Got a little rib trouble.'

'Hah,' Leo said, breathing a blast of pure alcohol in Blaine's face.

'Puff the Magic Dragon. If I lit a match you'd turn into a flame thrower.'

Leo sniffed, then turned and

shuffled back down the hall. Blaine followed along behind him, breathing hard. They went into Leo's surgery which, unlike its owner, was spick and span.

'Get up on the table,' Leo muttered.

'I can't. I'm in extreme pain.'

'What happened to you?'

'I was kicked by an ass named Alfred.'

'How do you know his name is Alfred?'

'He told me.'

Leo whistled through his teeth.

'A talking ass,' he said. 'Now I've heard everything.'

He went to a glass-fronted cupboard and took out a roll of surgical tape. 'Take off your jacket and shirt,' he instructed Blaine.

'The vest as well?'

'You're wearing a vest in the summer?'

'My mother told me never to leave my vest off until Mid-Summer's

Day.'

'Wise woman.'

Leo whistled again when he saw the purple bruising on Blaine's rib cage.

'Nasty,' he said, poking gently at Blaine's skin with a nicotine-stained finger.

'Easy, Leo, I think there's something broken in there.'

Leo nodded. He said, 'All I can do is tape you up. You need to go and get yourself X-rayed. And don't sneeze or yawn.'

'Why?'

'A splinter of rib could puncture your heart and do you in.'

CHAPTER FOURTEEN

'Jesus,' Blaine said when Leo had finished taping him up, 'I can't breathe.'

'You'll get used to it. Use your

47

ears, nose and arse. At least it improves your figure. Think of yourself as wearing a corset.'

'I feel as if I'm being squeezed to death by Hulk Hogan.'

'Listen,' Leo said, 'I'm using up valuable drinking time here. That'll be twenty quid.'

'Put it on my account.'

Leo went off grumbling, leaving Blaine to creak around the surgery like the Tin Man from *The Wizard of Oz*. After a while he got the hang of it. He went out into the hall and dropped some coins into Leo's pay phone. He dialled his house in Cabra. On the fourth ring, his wife Annie answered.

'Hello?'

'This is E.T., calling home.'

'Blaine, is that you?'

'It is indeed me. You're still there?'

'That's obvious, isn't it? What do you want?'

'To speak to Sam Carey. I presume you haven't run her off?'

'On the contrary. We're just into our third gin & tonic.'

'You're drinking my gin?'

'And your tonic. And having a pleasant conversation about the men in our lives: you in mine, her father in hers.'

'Don't compare me to her father.'

'What's wrong with your voice? You sound like a chipmunk.'

'I'm wearing a corset.'

'I always knew there was something odd about you.'

'A surgical corset. Sam's father's hard men gave me a kicking.'

'Good for them. I wish I'd been there to watch.'

'It hurts like hell.'

'Poor baby.'

'You're laughing at me.'

'I'll put Sam onto you. She could do with a good laugh as well.'

Blaine leaned against the wall, feeling sorry for himself. He was badly in need of some TLC—tender loving care.

Sam did sound sympathetic when she came on the phone: 'Annie told me that bastard had you beaten up.'

'There were at least five of them,' Blaine said. 'But I gave a good account of myself.'

'Good for you.'

'I need to know where your mother lives. I think it's important I talk to her.'

'Why?'

'Just an idea I have. I want to hear what she thinks of her ex-husband.'

'You better bring ear plugs. The last time I was in her company she told me he was Satan come up out of hell.'

'So, where does she live?'

'In Howth. Number Fifteen, Freemantle Hill. Just off the summit. You know where it is?'

'I'll find it.'

'She's a tough old bird.'

'You think she might give me another kicking?'

'Not a kicking. But she swings a

50

mean umbrella.'

'You'll wait in the house until I call again?'

'As long as the gin lasts.'

CHAPTER FIFTEEN

The sun was low in the west now, the sky a milky blue. Blaine drove slowly in the heavy evening traffic. Every time he took a breath, he felt as if a knife had been inserted under his ribs.

He turned off at Sutton Cross and took the winding road to Howth summit. He parked, got out and leaned against the bonnet of the car. The bay was full of heat haze, the city hidden behind it. Down below him, a fishing boat idled. It looked like a toy boat at that distance.

He lit a cigarette, but drawing the smoke into his lungs was like inhaling over broken glass. He

51

groaned out loud, and a woman walking her dog stopped to gaze at him.

'A broken heart,' he told her. 'My wife's left me.'

'For another man?'

'No, for another woman. It's all the rage nowdays.'

The woman hastily pulled on the dog's leash and took off. When she had put a good distance between them, she stopped and looked back. Blaine gave her a wave. He took another couple of puffs of the cigarette, then threw it away. A jogger came high-stepping up the hill and Blaine asked him if he knew where Freemantle Hill was.

'I do.'

'Could you give me directions?'

'I could.'

Blaine waited while the man did some on-the-spot running. He was a little guy, with curly hair and a Charlie Chaplin moustache.

'It's today I'd like to go there,'

Blaine said. 'Not next week.'

'Oh, sure. Back down the road, first left, then first left again. That's Freemantle Hill. Who are you calling on?'

'Gay Byrne.'

'He doesn't live there. He lives over near the Baily Lighthouse.'

'Not that Gay Byrne. This is another Gay Byrne. There must be thousands of them about.'

'Oh, well, have a nice day. What's left of it.' The jogger ran down the hill, his little legs pumping. Blaine envied him his freedom of movement. It felt as if his own ribs were on fire. He got back into his car and followed the directions he had been given. Freemantle Hill had some nice houses on either side of it. There was a smell of money about them.

Number Fifteen was about halfway down. It was a bungalow. It had a red-tiled roof and white-painted walls. It also had a lot of ground around it. Bushes, flowers, even a few statues of fellows and girls with very few clothes on.

Blaine parked his car in the gravelled driveway, then moved stiffly to the door and rang the bell. It chimed loudly, but no one came to answer it. He tried a couple of times more. Same result.

Curious, he moved around the side of the building. There was a swimming pool, with the bottom painted blue. There was no water in it. A deck chair stood in a patch of sunlight. It contained an oldish woman who, on first glance, appeared to be dead. Her eyes were half open, her head fallen to one side. But when Blaine approached the chair, she suddenly straightened up. 'Who the hell are you?' she asked him in a hoarse voice. 'Not another one of my husband's goons sent to do me in?'

CHAPTER SIXTEEN

'It's him I've come to talk to you about,' Blaine said. 'I presume you are Mrs Carey?'

'Don't mention that name around here. I use my maiden name, Murphy. If you're no friend of my ex-husband's, you can call me Mabel.'

Blaine stood just out of the patch of sunlight and looked at her. Her daughter Sam had told him her mother had a drink problem. But she looked in good shape in spite of this. Her hair was nicely styled, her make-up well applied, her figure still trim. She was wearing shorts and a flowered silk blouse. On the garden table beside her an ice bucket contained a bottle of white wine. There was also a packet of Player's Navy Cut cigarettes, an expensive lighter and Patricia Scanlan's latest novel.

'So, what do you want?' she now asked. 'I'll give you two minutes to speak your business. Then you're out of here.'

'My name is John Blaine. I'm a private detective and I've just come from your daughter Sam—'

'You mean Assumpta?'

'Yes, Assumpta. I don't know if you are aware of this, but your ex-husband is trying to get her to marry a very unsuitable person.'

'What do you mean, unsuitable?'

'Well, for starters, she doesn't love him.'

'Love is for the birds.'

'Maybe in your case, but not in hers.'

'Yes, I was unfortunate. Two husbands and both of them shits.'

'Was there not someone else?'

The woman shifted in the chair, then shaded her eyes to see Blaine better.

'You have been talking to my

daughter,' she said. 'It had to be Assumpta who told you about George Emerson.'

'A foreman who worked for your ex-husband?'

'Yes, the only good man I ever met in my life.'

'He died in an accident?'

'That's right.'

'Like the accident that happened to your first husband?'

'Almost exactly the same.'

'Fell into a cement mixer?'

'Yes.'

'Were they pushed?'

Mabel Murphy looked hard at Blaine.

'Nothing was ever proved,' she said.

'But you think they were pushed?'

'Not think, know.'

'You've proof of that?'

'Maybe. If I had why should I tell you?'

'To help your daughter. To get her out of your ex-husband's control, once and for all.'

The woman stood up from the chair. She gazed in the direction of the house, then looked back at Blaine.

'It's almost dinner time,' she said. 'Why don't you come in and eat? We can talk more. I might even tell you a few things.'

'Things that will help your daughter?'

'We'll see.'

CHAPTER SEVENTEEN

They went in and sat down at a table in a very tastefully furnished dining room. A sulky-looking woman about Mabel's age came in and served them soup.

'That's Breda, my companion and housekeeper,' Mabel explained when the other woman had gone back out. 'No point trying to talk to her. She hates everyone, especially me.'

'Then why do you keep her on?'

'Good help is very hard to find.'

Blaine took a sip of the soup, which was delicious.

'I notice you're moving rather carefully,' Mabel said. 'Is there something wrong with you?'

Blaine told her how Carey's men had beaten him up. She made sympathetic noises, but didn't seem surprised. They finished the soup, then moody Breda came in and took the plates away.

'Look at her,' Mabel said. 'She has a face on her that would turn milk sour.'

'I think she heard you,' Blaine whispered.

'Sure she did. Makes her hate me all the more. It's good to know where you stand with people.'

Blaine made a face, but before he could say anything further the sulky one came in with the rest of the food. Lamb chops, marrowfat peas, mashed potatoes.

'Plain food, but good,' Mabel said. 'Eat up.'

Blaine did his best, but the pain in his ribs soon defeated him.

'Do you mind if I smoke?' he asked. Mabel shook her head, so he lit up. He poured himself a glass of wine and its cool chill settled his stomach a little.

'To get back to what we were talking about before,' he said. 'You mentioned you had proof that your former husband, McMullen, and his foreman, George Emerson, were murdered.'

'Did I say that?'

'I believe so. Don't play around, Mabel. Your daughter's happiness is at stake.'

'She doesn't visit me very often.'

'Doesn't mean she doesn't love you.'

'I suppose not.'

Mabel took up some potato on her fork and held it in front of her. She said, 'Have you wondered how I can afford to live in a big house in a place like Howth? With all the trimmings?'

'Your ex-husband's money?'

'Correct. But parting him from it is like getting blood out of a turnip.'

'But you have a way?'

Mabel put the mashed potato in her mouth and chewed slowly. 'Pour me a glass of wine,' she said. Blaine did so, ignoring the twinge in his battered ribs as he handed it across the table.

'The day that McMullen died,' Mabel said, 'George Emerson was filming an advertising video. Shots of the construction site, of the half-finished building, that sort of thing. But when he took a look at it afterwards, what do you think he saw?'

'Maybe a shot of someone who looked like Carey doing something he shouldn't?'

'Exactly. Pushing poor old Willie

McMullen into that cement mixer. Plain as daylight.'

'Carey himself?'

'He didn't have the minders then that he has now.'

CHAPTER EIGHTEEN

Blaine grinned happily, in spite of the pain in his rib cage.

'And Emerson gave you the video?'

'He knew he was in danger. How right he was.'

'So, why didn't you go to the police with it?'

'And kill the goose that laid the golden egg? Both Willie and George were dead. I couldn't bring them back. If Carey was arrested, there was a good chance he would have got off. He's an expert at bribing people. Better for him to be hit where it matters most, in his wallet. I've been bleeding him dry for years.'

'So that's why his business is in such a bad state.'

'Probably.'

'And are you willing to let me use this information to help your daughter?'

'Why not? If it annoys Carey, then it makes me happy.'

'Listen, I've got to go,' Blaine said, rising carefully to his feet. 'If I hurry I should just catch Carey in his office.'

'I'd like to see his face when you tell him you know about the video.'

'You've got it hidden away in a safe place, I hope?'

'Breda keeps it in her knickers. I'd like to see the man who can get in there.'

Blaine laughed.

'You're joking.'

'You think so?'

He shook his head.

'Mabel, it was very good to meet you. Maybe one of these days I'll come back out and we'll get plastered together.'

'Any time, big boy. Just give me a bell so that I can put on my warpaint.'

As Blaine was turning to go, Breda came in with the dessert. He went as fast as his injured ribs would allow, just in case she threw it over him.

He made it to the Carey building in record time but the woman in the foyer was shutting up shop when he arrived.

'Carey still aboard?' he asked her.

'I've had orders not to let you in.'

'Give him a buzz. Tell him I've been out to see his ex-wife and that I know about the video.'

'I've forgotten your name.'

'Blaine, as in chilblain.'

The woman muttered into the intercom, then she nodded her head at the stairs. 'He'll see you,' she said.

Blaine shuffled up the stairs and along the corridor to the door of Carey's office. It was standing open.

Alfred was leaning against the wall just inside. He looked bored.

Carey was also on his feet, in front of his desk. And he looked worried.

'Don't say anything,' Blaine told him. 'I'll do the talking. And I'm not asking, I'm telling. You'll cut your daughter free. Allow her to lead her own life. And you'll give her a reasonable amout of money to keep her in the style she deserves. I'll leave you to settle that up with her. If nothing has been done in a week's time, I'll go to the police with my information. And I know where the video is. You're getting off lightly. Really you should be in prison.'

CHAPTER NINETEEN

Carey went red in the face. He looked as if something was caught in his throat. He coughed and spluttered. Then he managed to say,

'Get to hell out of here. I don't want to see your ugly mug ever again.'

'Likewise, I'm sure. But first a little something in writing.'

They agreed the terms of the deal, then Blaine made for the door. Before leaving, he turned to Alfred.

'No hard feelings,' he said, extending his hand. Alfred looked confused, gazing from his boss to Blaine and back again. Finally he reached out and took the offered hand. Immediately Blaine pulled him forward and head-butted him on the bridge of his nose. There was a meaty clunk. Alfred fell back against the wall, then slid slowly down it. He held his cupped palm under his nose to catch the blood. There was a lot of it. Wearily Blaine went down the stairs. His forehead was now as painful as his ribs. But in spite of the pain, he felt good. The satisfaction of a job well done, he told himself. And he still had one thousand two hundred and fifty pounds of Carey's money to help heal his various aches and pains. He went outside into the evening air, found a phone box and rang home. This time Sam answered.

'I was about to leave.'

'The gin all finished?'

'Just about.'

'I hope you're not heading for Artie's place.'

'No, I've a girlfriend who lives in Rathmines. She's putting me up for the night.'

'I've got good news. Your father has agreed to draw up a legal document saying he has no more control over you. And he's also going to give you a generous allowance to help you get settled.'

'Hey,' a delighted Sam shouted into the phone, 'how did you manage all that?'

'It's a long story and it'll keep till tomorrow. You've got my phone number. Ring me and we'll arrange to meet. Then I'll tell you everything. And by the way, it wouldn't be a bad idea if you visited your mother more often. Just to show her how much you love her.'

'I'll do that.' The girl made kissing sounds down the phone. 'You're a darling man. How can I ever repay you?'

'I can think of a way but maybe we'll wait till you're older.'

'I'm old enough.'

'Sure you are.'

'And life isn't a sad song any more, is it? Especially not with good people like you in it.'

'Get away with you. Go on up to Rathmines and forget about me. Live your life like a summer-hunting swallow.'

'Till tomorrow?'

'Yeah, yeah.'

Blaine put the phone down, but he was grinning in spite of his pain.

CHAPTER TWENTY

He left his car parked outside the Carey building and walked down to the Clarence Hotel and went inside. He asked the porter to ring a taxi for him. While he was waiting he went into the bar and had a large brandy. It bloomed like fire in his stomach. The taxi arrived and took him up to the Cabra Road. There were lights in the front windows and a familiar crock of a car was parked in the drive. He stood beside it and looked at the sky. There was a sliver of moon and stars were beginning to blink into view. A red glow lit up the horizon, promising another fine day tomorrow. He found his keys and opened the front door. Annie was standing in the hall, the nozzle of a Hoover raised like a gun. She was wearing an apron with 'Who Gives a Fig?' stencilled on the front, and green wellington boots.

'I like the gear,' Blaine said.

'It's what a cleaning woman would wear. That's how you think of me, isn't it?'

'I think of you in many different ways. That's only one of them.'

'Thanks very much.'

'You're the light of my life.'

'Aha, flattery will get you everywhere.'

'I love you.'

'But?'

'You're not the easiest person in the world to live with.'

'We all have our faults.'

Annie put down the Hoover and leaned against the wall. There was a fine film of sweat on her upper lip that Blaine would have liked to brush off with his tongue.

He said, 'We could try again. I can change. You can change. Forgive and forget.'

'Forgive maybe, but it's hard to forget.'

'Let's seize the moment. We could go upstairs and try to coax a sweet song out of the bedsprings.'

'And after that?'

'We'll live each day as it comes.'

'You think it'll work?'

'We can give it a bloody good try.'

Annie grinned, then she came forward into Blaine's arms.

'Careful with the ribs,' he warned her.

'You think they'll interfere with your performance upstairs?' she asked, looking concerned.

'You can lead and I'll follow on.'

They were halfway up the stairs when Blaine paused.

'Just one thing. Any chance you'd wear those green wellingtons in bed?'

'Oh, you are kinky!'